A Loch Gaoil Novella

Loch Gaoil Paranormal Romance Series

Table of Contents

Lake Dreamer
By S. E. Isaac
BLURB:

Loch Gaoil had been declared forbidden lands to humans for centuries. Rumors of mystical monsters living in Loch Gaoil circulated in the nearby towns. Bets were set and dares were made on who could survive jumping into the loch and treading the forbidden water. No man, woman, or child had been foolish enough to accept the challenges or dares.... until now.

• • • •

Killian Bridgestone was visiting his relatives in Scotland one childhood summer when he nearly drowned in the forbidden Loch of Gaoil. When he thought he had taken his last breath, the unexpected happened. A beautiful girl came to his rescue opening his eyes up to a whole new world.

Faridah Addair knew the rule of her people: *Never be seen by a human.* The rule was simple, yet, she had broken the rule in order to save a human boy from drowning. She knew what she did was wrong, but she couldn't let him drown. There was something about him that called to her heart and soul. He was different.

For breaking the rule, Faridah was punished and sentenced to guard the Chamber of Gaoil. As the hands of time ticked by, she never stopped thinking about the boy she saved. The boy who changed her life forever...

Killian and Faridah are now adults. Killian has gone back to Scotland in search of the girl in his dreams. When their paths cross, decisions must be made. Will Faridah follow her heart or will she follow the law of her people this time and remain unseen?

Don't miss any of the stories in the Loch Gaoil series. A standalone series featuring six paranormal romance tales bringing together the mystery and mystique of the world beneath the waves.

Lake Dreamer by S.E. Isaac
Ripples of Love by Josette Reuel
In Search of Loch Lilies by C.A. King
Depths of a Sailor's Heart by Crystal St. Clair
Colter's Cove by Mandi Konesni
Lady of the Lake by Rexi Lake

CHAPTER ONE

Faridah

Faridah Addair of Loch Gaoil left the realm of the mermaids and swam to the surface of the loch to have her morning look around. The sun had just broken over the horizon. The morning dew still dripped from the strands of grass. Creatures of the forest drank peacefully from the loch.

"Good morning!" Faridah called out to the animals. None of them scurried off from her sudden morning greeting. They were used to Faridah.

Every day since she was five, she had mischievously ventured out of her realm and into the loch. The loch and the forest surrounding it were forbidden grounds to humans. For centuries, humans believed the loch to be haunted by spirits and demons. Generation after generation the tales grew larger and larger. Even with the scary tall tales some humans meddled their way through the dense forest and to the loch's shores putting their fate into the loch's hands.

"Faridah," Maira, Faridah's second oldest sister said softly as she breached the water's surface directly in front of Faridah. Faridah gasped from fright and clutched at her chest. "Sorry."

"It's okay. You just caught me off guard," Faridah said sweetly. Maira smiled in reply.

Faridah had always wished she looked like Maira. Maira had silver eyes, which glistened in the sunlight. Her porcelain skin and straight, jet-black hair were a nice contradiction to each other. Her tail was rainbowed with purples, pinks, greens, and golds. She and Faridah were opposite in looks.

Faridah had tan skin despite growing up in the depths of the loch. Her eyes were bright brown and were often compared to those of wolves. Her tail was a combination of the colors lilac, pink, and silver. Her hair was brownish-red when dry and curled into ringlets.

"Why are you looking at me like that?" Maira giggled.

"Why can't I look like you?" Faridah sighed. Maira splashed water in Faridah's face and huffed.

"We've been over this, Faridah. You're beautiful. All the males find you attractive," Maira continued on. "I don't know why you can't get it through your thick noggin."

"You just say that because I bring you back goodies from my adventures," Faridah grinned. Maira rolled her eyes before wrapping her arms around Faridah.

"What am I going to do with you, Faridah? How will I ever get a husband for you, if you keep acting like this?"

"Maira," Faridah groaned.

Since Faridah's fifteenth birthday, suitors had come for her hand in marriage. Every day there was some new male she was being introduced to. There had been several nice males, but none of them called to her heart or soul. None of them were males she could see herself with forever.

"Father says there's a new suitor coming by to see you, today?" Maira said, releasing her hold on Faridah.

"A new one? Who?"

Maira pressed her lips together and shrugged. Two of her tell-tale signs she was lying.

"Maira," Faridah warned.

"Tiernan," Maira blurted excitedly. Faridah's eyes widened.

"Tiernan?" Faridah said in a hushed breath. Maira nodded with a huge smile on her face. "He's already married."

"You'd be his new wife. You'd be part of the harem," Maira smiled ear to ear, but Faridah barely noticed because Faridah began to only see red.

Part of the damn harem? Faridah shouted in her mind out of respect for her sister.

"I know it isn't ideal, Faridah, but you'd be taken care of." Maira placed her hand on Faridah's shoulder and squeezed gently. "You'd have a good life, Faridah."

"I understand," Faridah whispered. She didn't want to fight with Maira. It wasn't Maira's fault that Faridah had somehow popped up on Tiernan's radar. So, it was pointless to take it out on Maira.

"Have you seen any of *them*, today?" Maira asked moving her hand from Faridah's shoulder and looking around.

"No. I haven't seen a human in months," Faridah replied disappointedly.

Faridah and the other mermaids found humans fascinating. Mermaids had lots in common with humans since both species were able to breathe air and walk on land. However, their differences outweighed their similarities. Humans feared and hunted things that they did not understand. For this reason, the mermaid king declared centuries ago that it was forbidden for a mermaid to be seen by a human.

"Think they'll come back this summer?" Maira asked, looking at the wooden dock.

"I don't kn–" Faridah stopped talking when she heard the voices of boys.

"Quick. Hide," Maira called out before submerging herself into the water.

Faridah decided to hide in the thick gathering of reeds and lilies that were close by.

"Hey! I'm not a chicken!" One of the boys cried out in a crisp unfamiliar accent. Curiosity rose in Faridah and she couldn't help peeking her head out just enough to see where the boys were.

They stood on the dock. Six in total. They all dressed alike except for one. He appeared to be from a faraway place. He looked to be around her age– fifteen or so. He had dark brown hair and creamy-colored skin. He wore a blue T-shirt and brown pants. He was the most handsome human Faridah had ever seen.

Whoa, she thought as she continued staring at him.

"If ye' weren't chicken, ye'd jump in the water and find the maidens of the loch," the taller red-haired boy sneered at the boy Faridah had been looking at.

"Why the hell would I jump in there, when I can't swim, Fergus?" the handsome boy groaned.

"Killian's a chicken," the chubbier red-haired boy teased making all but one of the boys laugh at the handsome boy.

Faridah found herself balling her hands into fists. She didn't like the handsome boy being picked on. She didn't know the boy, yet, she couldn't help but feel protective of him.

"I'm not a chicken, fat ass!" Killian roared, ending the laughter of the others.

"Shut ye' geggie!" the chubby boy replied.

"Yeah, ye' dobber," Fergus snarled.

"I don't even know what that means!" Killian yelled. "You, Scotts, talk funny!"

"Ye' Americans always think ye' betta' than everybody else!" Fergus pushed Killian hard.

Faridah's heart pounded while worry washed over her as she watched Killian teeter on the edge of the dock. She had to bite her tongue to keep from screaming out his name. Everything inside her was telling her to go against the rule of their people and go to Killian.

Killian caught his balance. Faridah let out the breath she had been holding and waited with anticipation to see what would happen next. Faridah felt someone tugging at her tail beneath the water. Without looking, she knew it was Maira. Faridah gestured under the water with her hands for Maira to go away. There were a few more tugs and then Maira's hand disappeared off Faridah's tail.

"Eh! Knock it off before I tell ye' maws," the smallest boy warned.

"Ye' clipe!" the tall one shouted.

"I'm no clipe!"

"Ye' tattlin' on us. That makes ye' a clipe!" Fergus growled then pushed the short one.

Faridah grew annoyed by the bullies. She hated bullies. All her life she had always come to the aid of the underdog.

The boys began fighting each other. Curse words and fists went flying. The boys held back nothing.

"Silly boys," Maira whispered. Faridah hadn't noticed Maira emerge from the water.

"I like the one wearing blue," Faridah smiled.

"Faridah," Maira groaned. "He's a human boy."

"Doesn't matter. Something is calling to me, Maira."

"You have Tier–"

"No, Maira. I will not be part of some... some orgyfest," Faridah seethed. "Don't I deserve more than that?"

Faridah looked at Maira with tears in her eyes.

"Faridah," Maira said softly. "Please, don't cry."

"I won't cry. I refuse." Faridah took a deep breath and shook her head. "I'll make my own destiny. Find my soulmate."

"Faridah," Maira sighed. "That's not the way of our people. Father will select your husband."

SPLASH!

The splashing sound was followed by shouts of panic.

"Killian! Killian!" All the boys called out to Killian, who was fighting to keep his head above water.

"Oh no," Faridah whispered. She turned to swim toward Killian, but Maira snatched Faridah's hand.

"No, Faridah," Maira said sternly. "We cannot intervene with humans. It's against the rules. You know this."

"He's drowning, Maira," Faridah pleaded.

"No." Maira's voice was flat. "Let's go."

Faridah pulled out of Maira's grasp.

"Help! Help!" Killian cried out. His head submerged under the water making panic rise in Faridah.

"Killian!" the boys shouted.

"Do something?" The chubby boy shoved at Fergus.

"And be eaten by the creatures?" Fergus shrieked.

"Hurry! Help him, George!" the chubby boy said to one of the older boys.

Killian was still underwater. The water above where Faridah had last seen Killian was bubbling, but soon fell calm. Faridah's world froze.

"Killian," she whispered before diving under the water and swimming in Killian's direction.

Faridah saw his body sinking towards the bottom of the loch. His arms and legs frantically moved in an attempt to swim to the top. The harder he tried the faster he seemed to sink.

His eyes were squeezed tightly shut. His cheeks were puffed out, as though they were filled with air.

Faridah swam as fast as she could. When she reached Killian, she took hold of his hands. His eyes opened wide. Fear crossed his face.

"It's okay. I'll help you," Faridah said under the water. She smiled slightly. It was her attempt to show Killian she meant no harm to him.

Killian's arms and legs relaxed. He no longer looked scared.

Faridah began to swim to the top, pulling Killian along with her. She shortly stopped when she realized she would be seen by the other boys. She had already broken the rule of her people by allowing Killian to see her. She would be punished; however, being seen by all the boys would make her punishment harsher.

Killian began to panic again. His cheeks were no longer puffed out. His eyes drifted between open and closed. He snatched one of his hands from Faridah and clutched his throat.

He's dying.

Killian was drowning from water and Faridah was drowning from fear. The thought of Killian dying made her stomach knot. Her heart shattered at the thought.

Without another thought, she pressed her lips against his. She blew a breath into his mouth. He greedily sucked up the air she offered.

Their eyes locked on one another. Their lips remained pressed against each other. They shared breaths back and forth. Killian's body relaxed and he wrapped an arm around Faridah's waist. She gasped into his mouth at the sudden intimate touch. She gripped his shirt and pulled him closer to her.

Faridah's body was filled with warmth from his touch. She felt like everything in life came together at that moment and she never wanted it to cease.

As much as she wanted it to last forever, the moment came to a screeching halt when the sound of muffled screams snatched Faridah back to reality. The other boys were still panicking over Killian. She needed to get Killian back to the surface. She didn't want to let him go, but it was the right thing.

With great reluctance, she swam him towards the surface. With one last breath into his mouth, Faridah released him. His eyes widened. He began to panic. Faridah held his face gently then pressed a kiss to his lips and smiled.

Before she could change her mind, she pushed him up to the surface while keeping herself submerged. She continued to push him up by his feet until his head popped out of the water.

"Killian! He's there!" One of the boys shouted. Seconds later, Killian was pulled from Faridah's arms and out of the water.

She quickly swam over to the tall reeds and lilies. She lifted her head out of the water slowly, careful to not be seen or heard by the boys, who were busy crowding around Killian checking on him.

"Faridah," Maira groaned as she swam over to Faridah. "Father will not be pleased. You will be punished."

"Doesn't matter," Faridah whispered and looked at Killian. "All that matters is that he's safe."

CHAPTER TWO

Killian

Ten years later...

"Ye' out of your mind wanting to go back there," George, Killian's cousin, declared. "Ye' got your head in the clouds, lake dreamer. Did ye' not learn your lesson when we were teens?"

"Relax," Killian laughed. "I just want to take a look. It's not often I get to come to Scotland."

"Ye' go back to Loch Gaoil and you won't be leaving Scotland!" George shook his head, then took a drink of his beer.

"What's the big deal? You didn't seem to care going that summer," Killian frowned. George leaned in close to Killian.

"Since that day," George whispered then looked around the bar. His eyes settled on Killian once more. "There's a spirit there."

"A spirit?" Killian asked, causing several people around them to look at him. He gave them an apologetic look. When they returned to their business, Killian looked at George.

"Ye' a spirit," George said softly.

"What kind of spirit?" Killian chuckled.

"It wears a black robe. It's face ye' can't see. It's over seven feet tall... It's a spirit, Killian."

"Have you seen it?" Killian leaned closer to George. "Where have they seen it?"

"One question at a time," George grumbled. "You don't still believe that you saw..."

George looked around the pub then back at Killian.

"You still don't think you were saved by a beautiful mermaiden, do ye'?"

"Yep," Killian replied before taking a long drink from his beer stein. "Now, tell me more about the robed person. Where has it been seen?"

"Allow me," the pub bartender said leaning in on the bar counter. "They say it's the spirit of the loch. That a sin was committed so now the spirit collects souls of all those who come near Loch Gaoil."

"The spirit is made up of those souls," a large man declared slamming his beer stein on the counter. "The loch be haunted!"

The man's loud words caused heads to whip in their direction.

George groaned. Most likely from the nosey people who had interrupted his and Killian's conversation. George wasn't the type of guy to air his dirty laundry. He preferred to keep to himself.

"It's true! It be haunted!" A woman shouted somewhere in the back of the pub.

Killian's interest was piqued. He had left New York and headed to Scotland to search for the mermaid who had saved him. That summer, he had gone back to the loch in search of her. However, his search always came up empty-handed.

Now, he was older, had more resources, and more time to search for her. He knew it was a long shot, but he needed to see her. The mermaid who haunted his dreams with her beautiful face.

"What about the mermaid?" Killian asked.

"They consumed the souls of our people!" Someone shouted.

First, it was the spirit eating souls, now the mermaids? Killian mused to himself.

"Aye," the bartender nodded. "Legion says the face of the loch guardian can't be seen because it has no soul of its own."

"What about the mermaids?" Killian asked again before the bartender and the others went back to the faceless robe spirit.

"You mean freshwater sirens?" the bartender muttered.

Killian rolled his eyes. He knew that part of the legion wasn't true. He had met a mermaid and she had saved his life. She was definitely not a siren.

"This idiot plans on going up to the loch. Don't ye?" a woman asked, walking up to the bar.

She had dark curly hair that flowed down her back. She wore a flannel shirt, blue jeans, and a vixen-like smirk. There was something dark and warning in her green eyes.

"Only a foolish man would go near that loch," she smirked.

The woman made a shiver run up Killian's spine. If anyone was a siren, who led men to their doom, it'd be her.

"Helena, shouldn't you be eating the soul of your latest conquest?" A woman with a beautiful voice asked walking up to Helena.

Helena turned to the other woman and frowned briefly.

"Faridah," Helena acknowledged the other woman with a slight bob of her head. "I didn't realize you were here, too."

Killian turned to face the newcomer. His heart skipped several beats as he stared into beautiful hazel-green eyes.

The woman's hair was pulled up into a messy bun. She wore no make-up. Her lips were pink, luscious, and curved into a smile.

"Hello, Killian," Faridah said sweetly.

It's her.

"Hello," Killian replied coolly. He found it hard to breathe with his savior a mere few feet from him.

He had dreamed of this moment for the past ten years. He had pictured her and her perfect smile a million times. However, he didn't imagine that she'd be even more stunning.

"Killian?" George asked, leaning over to Killian. "You know Faridah? The beautiful Faridah?"

"We're old friends. Aren't we Killian?" Faridah smiled brightly.

Killian found it hard to speak so he nodded.

"We were just discussing the loch," the bartender smiled at Faridah.

"Killian?" Faridah said, grabbing Killian's attention. He looked away from the bartender and smiled at Faridah.

"Care to go for a walk?" she gestured at the door.

"Faridah," a brute of a man groaned as he walked up to her side.

The brute was tall and built like a brickhouse. His black hair was long. Most guys would look feminine with long hair. Not this guy.

Nothing about the brute was feminine. He had a square jawline. Piercing blue eyes that were currently locked on Faridah. Killian's fist balled. He didn't like the way the man was staring at Faridah.

Killian's anxiousness settled when he realized Faridah was looking at him, and not *Thor's* twin.

"He's not one of us," the man said quietly, but not quiet enough. Killian frowned.

Bastard, Killian cursed the cockblocking brute.

"Tiernan," Faridah rolled her eyes. "This doesn't concern you."

"Your father would not–" Tiernan's words were sliced short by Faridah's death look.

"We've been down this road, Tiernan," she growled. "Don't cross me."

Faridah's feistiness both caught Killian off guard and aroused him. He liked seeing her stand up to Tiernan.

"Faridah," Tiernan glared down at Faridah. Killian shot up out of his seat and walked over to the two.

"Mind your tone, when you talk to Faridah," Killan warned.

Faridah smiled, then turned to Tiernan. She stood on her tiptoes. Tiernan lowered his head allowing her to whisper in his ear. He sighed heavily, nodded then walked off, but not before he glared at Killian.

"Do you mind if I borrow Killian?" Faridah asked, looking at George.

"Not at all. Borrow him for as long as ye' like," George blurted. Faridah giggled slightly then held out her hand to Killian. All eyes were on Killian, who stood frozen in shock.

"What the hell are ye' waiting for?" George grumbled.

"I don't bite... in case you forgot," she teased.

Her teasing words broke Killian from his trance. He shook his head and chuckled before taking hold of her hand.

He looked down at their joined hands. Her hand was much smaller and softer than his. Her light pink nails stood out against his tan skin.

"This way," she said, leading them through the pub and to a U-shaped booth in the corner. "I know I said a walk, but you don't mind sitting and talking. Do you?"

"Not at all," Killian smiled.

Faridah slid into the booth. Once she was settled, Killian slid in on the other side.

His heart raced as he took in Faridah's beauty. He felt like a little kid, who was finally talking to his crush.

"How have you been, Killian?" she asked softly.

"I've been well. What about you?"

Her eyes saddened. They looked like they were filled with years of pain. They weren't the same mesmerizing cheerful eyes Killian had seen moments ago.

"Are you okay?" Killian asked concerned

"Yes," she whispered. "It's been a... long ten years."

She laughed softly, but Killian could tell it was forced. It was also filled with sorrow.

"Faridah," Killian reached across the table and took hold of her hand. She was ice cold and trembling. "Faridah, what happened?"

She looked down at their hands briefly. She took a deep breath then returned her gaze to Killian.

"Let's just say... my people were not happy with me saving you. Our people aren't to be seen by..." She looked around the pub. "Your kind."

Guilt struck Killian. Faridah had been punished because she had saved him.

That day had been the best day of his life. He had spent countless nights dreaming of her beautiful face. He couldn't see her, but he was still happy.

Not Faridah. She must've had nightmares from meeting him. Killian had been the cause of her pain.

"I'm so sorry. I never wanted you to get punished. If I had known that, I would have gone back with you and asked for the punishment," Killian sighed.

"That's sweet of you, Killian, but I doubt you could hold your breath that long," she teased.

The glimmer in her eyes returned. The emptiness in the pit of Killian's stomach filled with butterflies.

"Yeah. I couldn't even swim back then," he chuckled.

"Yes. I remember," she laughed.

"Did they hurt you?" he asked softly.

"I'm fine, Killian," she assured him.

"Faridah, I'm so sorry. If we hadn't gone down to the loch, none of this would have happened."

Killian couldn't help but feel responsible for it all. He hadn't been the one to suggest going to the loch; however, in the end he was the reason for her being seen by a human.

"Killian," Faridah said sliding closer to him with their hands still holding. "It's not your fault."

"You saved me, Faridah. If you hadn't, you wouldn't have gotten in trouble."

"And I'd do it again, in a heartbeat, Killian."

Killian wasn't a mushy kind of guy. At least he usually wasn't. Faridah changed that. He felt emotional with her. He wanted to hold her through the night. Watch sunrises and sunsets with her. He wanted to kiss her until they were both left breathless.

"What brought you back?" Faridah asked.

"Um..." Killian ran his free hand through his hair nervously. He didn't want to come across as a creeper.

Well, you see, Faridah. I flew thousands of miles to search for you.

"Just here visiting my cousin, George," he gestured back at the bar. George and a few others were staring at Killian and Faridah.

"Oh," Faridah breathed. She sounded disappointed. Killian turned and faced her.

"What's wrong?" He stroked the top of her hand with his thumb.

"Nothing," she smiled and shook her thought away. "It's just nice to see you again."

CHAPTER THREE

Faridah

Faridah could tell Killian wasn't buying her lie. He had seen right through her smile. She hadn't meant to sound so disappointed when he said he was only there to visit his cousin. She had just hoped that he had come to find her.

"How long are you here for?" she asked, changing the subject.

"Not sure, yet," he shrugged. "All depends."

On? Faridah wanted to ask, but her nerves were too high for her to be bold enough to ask.

"I'm surprised to see you here," Killian whispered. He gently squeezed her hand. "I mean, I thought only water."

Faridah burst into laughter.

Most people believed that mermaids couldn't go on land unless they fell in love with a human. And even then, they thought there had to be a true love's kiss.

"That's just a tale people have told over the years," Faridah whispered in his ear. She noticed him suck in a breath as she leaned away from him.

"I see," he cleared his throat. "How long can you be out of... you know?"

"As long as we want. We just need to submerge in water for an hour or so," she shrugged as though it wasn't a big deal to breathe underwater.

"I learned how to swim by the way," Killian chuckled.

"You can?" she asked excitedly, but her smile soon turned to a pout.

"What's wrong?"

"Since you know how to swim that means I won't be able to save you and steal a second kiss," she mused, making Killian laugh.

"I can always forget how to and fall in," he winked at Faridah. Her cheeks reddened and she toyed with her shirt.

How can he be so sexy?

"You're blushing," Killian smiled.

"I know. Sorry."

"I figured lots of guys...uh...men... mer..."

"Just *guys* is fine. No need for technicalities," she laughed.

"Okay. Got it," he nodded firmly and smiled. "I had figured all the *guys* wanted you and stole kisses.

Faridah shook her head, while trying to hold back her laughter.

"Did you think I was a kissing monster of the loch?" Faridah joked.

There were many rumors and tales about the loch. However, a kissing monster wasn't one she had ever heard. If there was a kissing monster, it definitely wasn't Faridah. She avoided the males of her kind in hopes that Killian would one day return.

Killian scooted directly next to her. His cologne wrapped around her like a blanket.

"I hoped you weren't, but as beautiful as you are. I'd understand if you were," he admitted.

"No kissing monster here." Faridah shook her head.

"That's good."

Faridah watched Killian's cheeks redden. She found his shyness cute. He was an extremely masculine man, yet, he looked vulnerable to her words.

A long silence fell over them. They stared at each other. Occasionally, Faridah would nervously smile.

She had dreamed of this day. She had years to think of what she'd say to him. The moment was here, and she had only managed to keep confidence for a few short minutes.

When Faridah had walked into the pub and saw Helena flirting, Faridah wondered who Helena's next victim was. Her heart skipped a beat. Her chest tightened and her knees grew weak. She couldn't believe her eyes. Killian was finally back.

Killian cleared his throat. Faridah shook away her thoughts and smiled.

"You okay?" he stroked the top of her hand.

"Yes. Just feeling a bit shy suddenly," she admitted in a whisper.

"Me too," he smiled. "I didn't think I'd ever find you."

"So, you were looking for me?" Faridah bit her bottom lip while she waited for Killian to answer.

He rubbed the back of his neck with his free hand. He looked around the room and took a few deep breaths. He looked back at Faridah.

"Can we meet tomorrow somewhere else?" he gestured with his free hand around the pub. "Somewhere quieter?"

"I guess this place is a bit loud." Faridah looked around. A good portion of the people in the pub were staring at them. "And super nosey," she groaned.

"Are you busy tomorrow?"

"I have a few things to do tomorrow morning, but after that I'm free."

For the past ten years as punishment for allowing Killian to see her, Faridah had been the responsibility of guarding the

Chamber of Gaoil. The Chamber of Gaoil was where Faridah's people were buried. It was an underwater tomb. Faridah spent all her days and nights in front of the large iron gates. The only ones of her kind that she saw were those paying respects to the dead. She could only speak to greet and farewell visitors and say the Gaoil prayer throughout the day.

It was Killian's face that kept her going.

CHAPTER FOUR

Killian

The look in Faridah's eyes made Killian's stomach knot. She looked sad. Whatever had her lost in thought was something that caused her pain.

"Faridah?" Killian whispered before kissing the top of Faridah's hand.

"Killian," she smiled.

"Are you okay?"

"Of course. The boy who couldn't swim has returned," she teased, making Killian chuckle.

"That I have. Returned to the homelands."

"Welcome back."

"Faridah, you are needed back," a burly man's voice said, breaking the moment between Killian and Faridah.

Killian looked up to see two oversized men with no facial hair, chiseled jaws, and muscles that would intimidate the gods.

"Tiernan told, I suppose?" Faridah groaned.

"Aye," the pale-skinned man nodded.

"Sorry, Faridah," the dark-skinned man offered with a remorseful look.

"I'll be outside shortly," Faridah sighed then looked across the room at Helena. "Tell Helena she must return as well. I don't want her near Killian," Faridah ordered.

"As you wish," the two men chuckled then made their way over to Helena. Helena turned quick on her heels and glared at Faridah. Killian saw a look on Faridah's face that made him want to kiss her senseless. She was marking her territory with Helena.

"You two seem close," Killian joked.

"Best friends," Faridah looked at him. "Before I'm taken away, where should we meet tomorrow?"

"Are you sure that's a good idea? I don't want to get you in–"

Faridah's soft lips pressed against his lips. She slowly pulled away. The kiss was over before he knew it but left him greedy. He wanted to explore her mouth with his tongue.

"When can I see you, Killian?" Faridah asked again. This time she smiled ear to ear.

"Give me a time and place. I'll be there," Killian laughed.

The last thing he wanted was to get Faridah in trouble. However, he couldn't tell her *no*, even if he wanted to. He'd just have to have faith that the gods would be on their side this time.

"The same place we first met, at noon?" she asked. Killian took in her look of hopefulness.

"I could never deny you, Faridah." Killian stroked her chin with his free hand. Her eyes closed briefly. When she opened her eyes, they were brighter, almost glowing green.

"Your eyes being bright... does that mean you're happy?"

Faridah's eyes widened. She shook her head then looked around the room nervously.

"This is your fault," she whispered.

"How so?" Killian asked with an eyebrow raised.

"Meet me tomorrow and I'll tell you." She kissed him swiftly then made her way out of the pub.

"Tomorrow at noon," Killian repeated to himself. He groaned when he realized she had given a time.

Do they even have clocks down there?

CHAPTER FIVE

"Was that the human, who got you cast out?" Tiernan asked, leaning against one of the pillars of the Chamber of Gaoil. He crossed his arms in front of his chest.

Faridah took in Tiernan's good looks. His long black hair flowed around him. His blue eyes were like sapphires and shimmered every so often when the sun's beams made their way under the water. His body was nearly perfect. He was rock solid, and all the other female mermaids swooned to get his attention.

Faridah's life would be much easier if she just accepted Tiernan's proposal. She wouldn't be the guardian of the Chamber of Gaoil. She'd be pampered and want for nothing. But her heart wouldn't allow her to settle for Tiernan. Her heart belonged to Killian. Seeing him at the pub had only confirmed her feelings.

"Faridah, what does the human have that I don't? What can he offer you that I can't? Tell me so I can improve myself," Tiernan said pushing off the pillar and swimming close to her.

"Haven't you suffered enough?" he asked, stroking her cheek softly. His touch did nothing for her; not like Killian's touch.

"Tiernan," Faridah's eldest sister, Lola, called out. Tiernan quickly lowered his hand to his sides.

Lola swam over to Faridah and Tiernan. Lola's wavy red hair flowed behind her like a river of crimson. Her icy blue eyes were locked on Tiernan as was her frown.

"Faridah has a duty at the Chamber of Gaoil," Lola scolded. Lola's ladies-in-waiting, who stood behind Lola, nodded in agreeance. "I'm sure Faridah is honored that a mer like you is interested in her. However, this isn't the time nor the place."

Faridah was thankful for Lola's interruption. Tiernan could talk until he was blue in the face and Faridah wouldn't be able to stop him because she was bound by duty to remain silent. Tiernan knew this, which is why he showed up the same time every day to confess his feelings to Faridah.

"Tiernan, I would like a moment with my sister," Lola gestured at the exit to the chamber's hall. Tiernan nodded his head.

"Yes, Your Highness," he said, then turned to Faridah.

"Faridah, we'll continue our talk later," he smiled then left the Chamber of Gaoil.

"That dobber," Lola muttered, making her ladies in waiting giggle. Faridah steadied her mind to keep from laughing. She remained straight-faced.

"I'll assume that it's true, Faridah. The human boy is now a man, and has come to find you," Lola gushed. She held her hands to her heart.

Out of all Faridah's sisters, Lola was the most romantic. The most compassionate. And, the one who stood up for Faridah the most. Lola was like a second mother to Faridah. Someone Faridah could always confide in.

"I'm all warm and tingly inside, Faridah," Lola smiled and twirled. The water held Lola's hair making it look like it was in slow motion. When Lola stopped twirling, she swam over to Faridah.

"You deserve to be happy, Faridah," Lola sighed. "Your punishment for saving him was unjust... yet, you endured it for him. Isn't that romantic, Cora?" Lola looked over her shoulder at Cora, Lola's favorite lady in waiting and Lola's husband's sister. Cora had tended to Lola even before Lola married Chibale.

Cora was a beautiful exotic mermaid, who came from Africa. Her skin was a beautiful ebony color. Her amber-colored eyes always drew Faridah in. Cora's thick black hair made all other female mermaids green with envy.

"Truly romantic, Your Highness," Cora smiled at Faridah.

Faridah wasn't sure if Cora was addressing Lola or Faridah with the title. Either way, Cora's words sounded genuine.

"Maira is working on mother and father. You know how passionate she gets when she talks about fate and destiny," Lola giggled. "Maira agrees with me. The human is your anam cara."

Anam cara? Faridah wondered to herself.

All this time, the thought never crossed Faridah's mind. She had just known she felt a connection to Killian. She never thought that the reason she felt the way she did towards Killian was because they were destined anam caras.

"Oh, Faridah," Lola sighed. "You've been too busy floating in the clouds to see that Aonghus has graced you."

"Mother and father won't go against the will of a god," Lola hummed.

The sunlight from above beamed through the Chamber of Gaoil and down onto the Soul Keeper. The Soul Keeper illuminated the entire chamber. Faridah, Lola, and the ladies in waiting lowered their heads out of respect to the gods and to those souls locked away within the Soul Keeper.

"The gods and goddesses of our people swim beside you as you take the journey to Caelum," Faridah chanted softly in their native Mer language.

It wasn't until the Soul Keeper's light dimmed that everyone raised their heads and said, "Gabh fois gu sìtheil."

CHAPTER SIX

Killian

Killian walked slowly through the dense forest that surrounded the loch. His nerves were sky-high as he made the trek to meet Faridah.

After Faridah had left the pub, George had nagged Killian for details. George wanted to know how Killian knew the gorgeous Faridah. Killian spent hours trying to dodge George's evasive question. In the end, George didn't get his answers and Killian got no sleep.

"Damn you, George," Killian yawned.

When Killian finally broke through the tree line, he was able to see the dock. Sitting on the edge of the dock with her feet in the water was Faridah. She looked over her shoulder at Killian and smiled.

She looked like a goddess. The wind blew her red hair slightly, while the sun beamed down on her. She wore a floral print dress with thin straps.

"So damn beautiful," Killian smiled then walked to the dock and sat next to Faridah.

"I was beginning to think you weren't coming," Faridah laughed.

"Am I that late?" Killian quickly looked at his watch. *12:15.*

"I'm really sorry," he groaned.

"It's okay. I was just giving you a hard time." She bumped him playfully with her shoulder making him laugh.

"You can thank my cousin for my tardiness," he admitted. Faridah's eyebrow rose. "He kept me up all night trying to figure out how I knew you and what we talked about."

"Ah. I see," she smiled. "What'd you tell him?"

"Wasn't sure what to tell him." Killian looked out across the loch. "I've talked about that day for years to him. Told him about the beautiful mermaid who saved me. He thought I was nuts for coming here to search for you... I guess I kind of am," Killian chuckled.

"You came to find me?" Faridah asked in a whisper.

Killian felt like an idiot for admitting his reason for coming to Scotland. She probably thought he was a creepy stalker now.

"Yes," he admitted softly in defeat.

"That makes me happy."

Killian looked at Faridah. She was smiling bashfully. She glanced at him, but quickly looked away and at the water.

"I'd always hoped you'd come back." Her words were faint out loud but booming in Killian's mind. She had wanted to see him again. "Did you tell your cousin that I'm the mermaid?"

"No," Killian blurted. "I mean, no. I didn't tell him. You've suffered enough."

"Thank you," she looked at him and smiled.

Silence fell over them. There gazes locked on each other, but not a word spoken. There were a thousand things that Killian wanted to ask and say to Faridah. He just couldn't find the words. Not with her sitting so close to him and looking at him. His nerves had him in a trance.

"Killian, say something. You're too quiet," Faridah finally said.

"Sorry." Killian offered her an apologetic smile. "All this seems surreal."

"I know," Faridah laughed. "I still can't believe you're here."

"Me either."

A gust of wind blew. Faridah's hair flowed around her before settling. Strands were now in her face. Without thought, Killian brought his fingers up to her face and swept her hair behind her ear. She smiled. Killian began to bring his hand down, but Faridah held it against her face.

"The boy who couldn't swim," she mused. Killian stroked her cheek with his thumb and laughed. "When will you know when you are going back home?"

Guilt struck Killian. He had an entire life back in New York. A life he put on hold to come to Scotland.

"Not too sure," he sighed. Faridah brought his hand down to her lap. She held it with both her hands.

"I could always kidnap you," she grinned.

"Kidnap me?" Killian laughed. "Can't kidnap the willing, sweetheart."

He should have felt embarrassed for his comment. He should have apologized for calling her *sweetheart.* The nerves he had felt were gone. They had left when she took hold of his hand and held it to her face.

"Good," she squeezed his hand gently. "Makes it easier to keep you."

"Is that your plan, Faridah?" Killian asked huskily. He watched her take a deep breath. Her cheeks reddened. Her fingers fidgeted with his.

"I mean, I... I wouldn't mind keeping y–"

Faridah stopped talking and looked down at the water. She groaned then looked at Killian.

"They're coming," she sighed. "Are you staying at an inn or with your cousin?"

"An inn."

There was no way in hell he was staying with George and his family. George had four children, who were all under the age of six. His wife tended to nag George constantly. Killian wanted to enjoy his vacation without having to listen to loud children or a nagging wife. Plus, George snored like a chainsaw.

"Can we go there? Or maybe the coffee shop?" Faridah asked while frowning at the water.

"Is someone there?" Killian leaned forward to have a better look at the water. The water was still. He saw nothing but a few water lilies and a dragonfly. He looked at Faridah.

"My sisters are coming to be nosey," she groaned.

"Sisters?"

Killian couldn't believe that Faridah had sisters; beautiful ones at that. He couldn't help but wonder if they were just as beautiful as her.

He looked over at Faridah and smiled.

No one can compare to her.

"What are you smiling about?" she asked, cocking her head to the side.

"Just thinking how there's lots I don't know about you," he lied.

"And there's lots I don't know about you either."

"How many sisters do you have?" Killian looked down at the water just as a head rose from the water. He yelled then jumped to his feet pulling Faridah up with him. He placed her behind him. Three more heads appeared from the water.

"Relax, Killian," Faridah giggled.

"She has four sisters," a sweet woman's voice laughed. "I would be Princess Lola, eldest of the Addair sisters."

Killian looked again at the four heads that had appeared. They weren't monsters at all. They were all beautiful women – mermaids. They had similar features to Faridah.

The mermaid who spoke had bright red hair and piercing light blue eyes. She looked fierce, yet her voice was gentle.

"I am Princess Maira, second eldest of the Addair sisters," the mermaid with silver eyes, pale skin, and jet-black hair smiled.

"I am Princess Grace, third eldest of the Addair sisters," the mermaid with purple eyes, tanned skin, and thick brown hair giggled. She swam closer to the dock and looked up at Killian. "I see now why Faridah risked it all for you."

"Grace!" the group of women shouted. Grace pouted then swam over to Lola, who scolded her.

"And, last but not least," a woman laughed. "I am Princess Isla, second youngest of the Addair sisters."

The mermaid who spoke had beautiful dark skin. Her hair was braided halfway back with the rest of it flowing down. Her eyes were hazel. Out of all the sisters, Isla and Faridah looked the most related.

"It is nice to meet you, Lola, Maira, Grace, and Isla," Killian said. He looked at each mermaid as he said her name. "I am Killian."

"Pleasure is ours," the mermaids said in unison.

"Okay. You've met him. Be on your way," Faridah stepped in front of Killian and shooed her sisters. The four mermaids didn't budge. They only smiled up at Faridah.

"I think we deserve to meet your anam caras," Grace smiled.

"Anamma... what?" Killian asked.

"Ah! Nothing!" Faridah screamed and covered his ears with her hands. She looked over her shoulder back at her sisters. Killian couldn't see Faridah's face, but her sisters looked amused so he could only assume that she was glaring.

"Faridah," Killian whispered and lowered her hands. He held her hand. "I don't mind meeting your sisters."

"Ooo. I like him," Isla said, pulling herself up onto the dock.

Killian's eyes widened at the sight of her dark red and green tail. The tail began to morph into legs as did the scaled bra that covered her large breasts. Isla was now sitting on the dock naked.

"Whoa," he breathed.

"Isla!" Faridah screamed then pushed Isla back into the water. Isla stuck her head out of the water. Faridah hissed loudly at her sister and stood in front of Killian.

"What the hell, Faridah?" Isla snapped.

"You think being exposed to Faridah's anam cara would go over well?" Lola laughed.

"My apologies, Faridah," Isla sighed. "I was just super excited and thoughtless."

"It's okay, Isla," Faridah whispered. The tension in her shoulders dropped and she sighed heavily. "This is all... overwhelming."

"Why don't we all go out for coffee? My treat," Killian offered. "We could meet there that way you all can find some..."

Killian didn't know if he should keep speaking or not. He didn't want to offend them by telling them to go throw some clothes on and then come find him. After all, they were Faridah's sisters and princesses of the loch.

Princesses? The titles the mermaids had said while introducing themselves finally registered in his mind. He had been too focused on their appearances and comparing them to Faridah.

"Princesses?" he whispered. Faridah's sisters laughed, while Faridah groaned. Her shoulders slumped. "You're a..."

He let his sentence fade off. Everything was surreal. Faridah wasn't just a mermaid from the loch, she was a princess of the loch. A princess had saved him. And, she had been punished because of him.

If her kind were willing to punish a princess, what would they do to a human who was in love with that princess? Would they punish Faridah again?

"Perhaps, it was a bad idea for me to come here," he finally said. "I don't want to cause any more trouble than I have."

"No!" Faridah's sisters yelled at him.

"There will be no trouble, Killian," Grace assured him.

"So, you will not leave our Faridah," Maira pointed her finger at him. "If you do, I will make sure that the Spirit of the Loch haunts you for eternity."

"Spirit of the Loch?" Killian asked looking over at Faridah.

"Don't worry. We won't let the spirit harm you," Faridah smiled, but her words weren't very reassuring.

"Speaking of the Spirit of the Loch," Isla groaned and pointed off in the distance. Killian looked where she was pointing.

A hundred feet away or so stood a tall figure in a black robe. Killian couldn't make out the face, but he couldn't help but feel that it was staring at him. When the robed figure began to move in their direction, hovering above the grass, Killian swallowed the invisible lodge in his throat.

"Um... am I safe?" he asked with his eyes locked on the spirit. Truth be told, he was afraid to look anywhere else.

"Looks like you're going for a swim, Killian," Lola mused.

"I am?" Faridah's sisters nodded in response. "Is there somewhere I can leave my phone and keys?"

"You have a spirit coming for you, and you're worried about your belongings?" Maira laughed. "You are a strange man, Killian."

"Aye. That he is," Grace agreed. "Into the water, Killian. We'll take you with us to father. Then he can tell the spirit that no harm is to come by you."

"Father?" Killian choked.

It was one thing for Killian to meet Faridah's sisters. The thought of meeting her father made him want to run for the hills. Killian and Faridah weren't an item. They were just catching up after ten years. There wasn't a reason to meet him.

"Don't be a chicken," Isla laughed.

"I just remembered that I'm supposed to meet up with George for a few pints," Killian rambled as he ran his hands through his short hair. "I'll meet you in town, Faridah." He headed away from her and down the dock.

Killian was a cage fighter, who was brutal in the cage. Yet, he was hightailing it away from the loch because he couldn't handle the thought of meeting Faridah's father. The king of the loch. All the guys Killian had fought against. All the punches Killian had taken. None of those things would compare to having Faridah's father's eyes looking at him from his throne.

"Great. Took me ten years to find him! And took you all three minutes to scare him off," Faridah shouted at her sisters. Killian came to a halt, sighed and turned to face her. Her back was to him.

"It's not their fault, Faridah," Killian sighed again then walked over to her. She slowly turned and faced him. "Meeting your dad wasn't on my to-do list... ever. Honestly."

"It's not on mine either," she admitted softly. She looked over Killian's shoulders and her eyes widened. "However, there's no choice now. The spirit is here for you."

Killian looked over his shoulder. The robed spirit hovered over the far-end of the dock.

Fuck. Killian cursed in his mind as he stepped in front of Faridah, so she was behind him and away from the spirit.

"You're really dense, Killian," Maira griped. "The spirit is here for you not Faridah."

"Push him in Faridah. We need to get him to safety," Lola ordered. Killian heard Faridah mutter something under her breath.

"Going to have to jump, Killian," Faridah said, grabbing his arm. He looked down at her.

"I said I could swim, not hold my breath for eternity, Faridah," he complained, making her laugh.

"Then it's a good thing I can," she teased before pushing him into the water.

CHAPTER SEVEN

Faridah

Faridah jumped into the water. Her body morphed back into its mermaid form. She swam up to Killian and smiled. He wiped the water from his face.

"You know this is a crazy idea, right?" he sighed. "I could have just gone back to town and the spirit would leave me alone. Right?"

"I'm sorry, Killian," she offered a small smile. "We'll help you get back to town if that's what you wish." Her sentence finished in a whisper.

"I'm just not sure how your kind will handle a human being in your world," Killian said, treading water.

"Our kind has to accept you as Faridah's anam cara, Killian," Lola rested her hand on his shoulder gently.

"What exactly is an anam cara?" He looked around between Faridah and her sisters. Faridah's sisters were all looking at her. Faridah's stomach knotted and she felt like she would be sick. "Faridah? What is an anam cara?"

She wanted to come clean with Killian; however, she wanted time for herself to digest the idea of them being anam cara. Her sisters had ruined the opportunity for Faridah to discuss it with Killian. Her sisters were old-fashioned. Fate was as it was. There was no questioning it.

Most humans weren't like that. They needed time to find their soulmate. They needed reasonings to explain their feelings towards another human. How would Killian understand that he and Faridah were soulmates?

"Follow me. We'll get out of the water over there and I'll help you leave the forest," she blurted.

"No," Grace said firmly. "Father and he need to talk."

"We can't force our ways on him," Faridah fired back.

"There's no time for arguments," Isla interrupted. "The spirit is here." Isla pointed at the dock where the spirit now hovered over the edge.

"I'm sorry, Killian," Faridah whispered before grabbing his hand and pulling him under the water.

Killian's body tensed as they swam deeper toward the bottom of the loch. Faridah gestured for her sisters to go ahead of them. They nodded and then swam to the barrier that would lead to their realm.

Faridah took Killian's face in her hands. He looked at her and she smiled letting him know that he was safe with her. His body relaxed. She brought her lips to his and blew a deep breath into his mouth before leading him down to the barrier and through it.

When they resurfaced from the water, they were no longer in the Loch of Gaoil. They were in the realm of Faridah's kind. Killian was now surrounded by mermen and mermaidens of all sizes and colors.

Killian's eyes were wide as he took in the new world around him. He would open his mouth to speak, but quickly close it as his attention was diverted to something else. He looked like a child in a candy shop.

"This is only one of the marketplaces of our kind, Killian," Lola said pointing at different vendors. "It's not too much different from where you are from. There are goods we buy, trade, or sell."

"I see this," Killian whispered, looking around at various things.

"We need to travel to the castle. You will need to hold your breath again. Are you ready?" Maira asked him. Faridah watched as Killian paled. She couldn't blame him for being nervous. He was not only in a new world, but he was about to meet the king of the seven seas.

"I'm right here," Faridah smiled then held his hand with both of hers. "My sisters and I will protect you," she teased, hoping to make him laugh. When he gave her a smile, she felt the tension in her own body leave.

"As long as you ladies will protect me," he chuckled.

"We will. Come on, land legs," Isla laughed then submerged under the water.

"Don't take offense, she jokes with everyone," Grace sighed before going under the water.

"She's right. Now come on... land legs," Faridah giggled.

"Oh. Not you too?" Killian shook his head and smiled. "I'm in for a world of trouble, aren't I?" He asked Lola.

"You have no idea," Lola smiled. "Come along."

Soon, they were under the water again. Faridah held one of Killian's hands and led him through the water toward the castle. He would squeeze her hand when he was running out of air. She'd blow into his mouth and they'd continue their journey.

Faridah watched Killian as he took in the city full of her people. When the castle came into view, his eyes widened and his face paled. Faridah reassured his safety and that everything was okay by squeezing his hand softly. He looked at her and smiled.

At the castle steps, Faridah blew one more time into Killian's mouth before they entered the castle. The guards bowed as

Faridah, her sisters, and Killian swam by. Nerves rose in Faridah the closer they got to the throne room.

Her father was traditional. He had wanted his daughters to all marry into prestigious families. Faridah's mother on the other hand didn't care who her daughters married as long as they gave her grandchildren. Her mother had harped on Faridah about how Faridah and Tiernan would make beautiful children.

The two large doors leading to the throne room opened up allowing Faridah and the others to swim inside. The room was filled with the council. All eyes turned to face Faridah and them. Her father sat on his throne with his eyebrow raised. Her mother sat on her throne beside her father with a small smile. Everyone in the room wore their formal burgundy-colored robes.

"Daughters," Faridah's father groaned.

"Father," Faridah and her sisters said together.

Killian squeezed Faridah's hand letting her know he was running out of air. Heat rose in Faridah's cheeks when she realized she would have to breathe into his mouth in front of her parents and the council. Killian squeezing her hand firmer making her lose all shyness. His safety was more important.

She pressed her lips against his and breathed into his mouth. Gasps filled the room.

"Father, may I introduce Faridah's anam cara, Killian," Lola said cheerfully. Several of the council gasped. Faridah's parents' eyes widened. They exchanged looks back and forth then looked at Killian.

"You are the *human* Faridah saved?" Faridah's mother asked. Killian nodded his head. "Ah. I see." She looked at Faridah and smiled.

"He can't hold his breath much longer, father," Faridah looked at her father, who nodded.

"Go to your rooms and put on your robes," her father ordered. "Leave the human–"

"Killian," Faridah interrupted. She usually wouldn't have cut her father off, but she didn't like Killian being referred to anything other than his name.

"Yes. Leave...*Killian* here." Her father rolled his eyes then gestured for his daughters to leave. Faridah blew one last breath into Killian's mouth, smiled and left the room along with her sisters. Faridah filled with guilt as the throne room doors closed behind her. She was leaving Killian to face her parents alone.

CHAPTER EIGHT

Killian

Killian's heart pounded as he heard the doors close. He was left to the wolves with no way out. Killian felt like Faridah's father's vibrant blue eyes were piercing through him. Her mother smiled at Killian, but even her sweet smile scared him. He was out of his comfort zone.

Faridah's father raised his hand and made a gesture. Killian thought for sure the signal was for the guards to take Killian and lock him away. When the water began to drain from the room and reached a level beneath his chin, he gasped for air. A sense of relief washed over him.

"Welcome to our kingdom," Faridah's mother smiled.

"Thank you, Your Majesty," Killian replied nervously and bowed.

"I do not recognize your dialect," Faridah's father stated making Killian stand tall and stare at the king.

"I am American, Your Majesty."

"Ah. I see," the king nodded. "Do all Americans not know how to swim?" The room filled with laughter, except for the queen who glared at the king. The king smiled smugly.

"Lessons were learned that day. I now know how to swim, Your Majesty," Killian chuckled. To Killian's surprise, the king laughed.

"Good because you caused quite a wave in our realm and to Faridah."

Killian felt remorse at the thought of what Faridah went through because of him.

"I apologize wholeheartedly to you both. I never meant to cause Faridah suffering. I swear," he assured Faridah's parents.

"I'm sure you speak the truth, Killian," the queen smiled. "You have returned to Scotland for Faridah?"

Killian's cheeks burned with embarrassment. He hadn't even told Faridah that she was the reason he came back to Scotland. Now, her parents were staring him down wanting to know the truth.

"Truthfully..." Killian took a deep breath and ran his hands through his hair before continuing. "Yes. I came back here to find her... Your Majesties."

"What reason do you have for coming to the castle?" the king asked.

"Your daughters were hoping you could talk to the spirit, so it doesn't try to eat me or what not, Your Majesties."

The king's head fell back, and he erupted with laughter. The queen seemed to be holding back a laugh and several people behind Killian laughed. Killian suddenly felt like an idiot. Everyone's amusement made Killian feel like an idiot.

"The spirit would not have eaten you, Killian," the queen said in a soft motherly tone.

"Oh," Killian whispered.

"The queen is right. Once the spirit realized who you were, it would have brought you to me, as I instructed. No harm would have come to you," the king said to Killian. "A nagging feeling told me that you would one day return."

"The princesses have returned, Your Majesty," a guard announced.

"Have them wait," the queen looked at the guard. "I wish to speak to Killian without them."

"Yes, Your Majesty," the guard replied. Killian looked at the queen.

"Are you willing to accept the fact you are Faridah's anam cara?" she asked Killian softly.

"I'm not sure what that is, Your Majesty?" Killian rocked back and forth on his feet.

"Get the hum– Killian a chair," the king ordered. Despite himself, Killian smiled at the king correcting Killian's name. The king didn't strike Killian as a man– merman –who was one to be told what to do or say.

A chair was offered to Killian. Killian thanked the person before taking a seat.

"Anam cara is what humans refer to as a soulmate," the queen began. Killian felt his stomach knot at the word *soulmate.*

"He's looking green behind the gills," the king laughed. The queen glared at the king then smiled at Killian.

"Our kind believes in fate, Killian. Faridah was punished for being seen by you; however, now that you have come back for her then fate must wish for you two to be together," the queen continued.

Killian felt like the room was spinning. Everything was coming at him too fast. He had come to Scotland in hopes of seeing Faridah again. He never imagined that he would be told that he was Faridah's soulmate or that they were bound by fate. Truth be told, Killian never thought that a relationship between him and Faridah was possible.

"What does an anam cara consist of, Your Majesties?" Killian asked quietly.

"You will become one of us and marry Faridah," the king boasted.

"One of you?" Killian choked.

"Yes. One of us," the king frowned. "Is there something wrong with becoming one of us?"

"No. Not at all. Just caught me off guard," Killian blurted, in fear of insulting the king and queen.

Soulmate. Become a mermaid. Sure. No big deal, Killian groaned to himself. He wondered what he had gotten himself into. He pinched himself to ensure he wasn't dreaming or maybe he did it in hopes that he was dreaming.

"Which part bothers you?" the king growled.

"Relax," Killian heard the queen whisper to the king. "This is a lot for him to take in." The king rolled his eyes and looked at Killian.

"Would you be willing to become one of us and marry Faridah?" the king asked flatly.

Killian swallowed hard. He wanted to run out of the room and hightail it back to his room back at the inn. But, even if he ran out of the room, he'd still be in their kingdom with no clue how to get back to the inn.

"Faridah and I haven't really spent much time together, Your Majesty," Killian finally managed to say. "It's not that I wouldn't eventually be willing to. I'm just overwhelmed by it all. As humans we date before commitment."

"Then you do not believe in fate?" the queen asked with her head cocked slightly.

"Honestly, I never really thought much about fate. Over the past decade, I've just thought about Faridah and nothing else," Killian admitted. The queen's disappointed look vanished and she smiled. "We will give you a few days to spend with Faridah before you make your decision."

"Um... Thank you." Killian wasn't sure what else to say.

"So be it," the king groaned.

"You will stay in Faridah's room and get to know one another," the queen announced, making Killian's eyes widen. He couldn't believe that the queen was willing to let Faridah and him share a bedroom.

"If she becomes pregnant there will be negotiations, you *will* marry Faridah," the king growled and pointed at Killian.

"Agreed," the queen nodded. "However, if you give me a grandchild, you will be forever in my favor," she smiled sweetly.

Soulmate. Marriage. Child. Those three words swirled in Killian's mind like a tornado.

CHAPTER NINE

Faridah

Faridah sat next to Killian on her bed. He hadn't said anything since they had left the throne room upon her father's orders. The tension in the room was almost unbearable, but Faridah remained quiet. Her fingers nervously fidgeted with her robe.

"Your parents seem nice," Killian said faintly. Faridah glanced at him and nodded.

"They are fair," she whispered.

"They are giving me a few days to decide." He ran his hands through his hair.

"To decide?" Faridah turned to face Killian. He stared straight ahead out the window into the sea. "Decide what Killian?"

"The whole anam cara thing," he sighed heavily.

Faridah felt her world come crashing down. Worry filled her of what her parents had said to Killian in regard to anam cara. She had wanted a chance to speak with Killian alone before any of the anam cara was brought up. When her sisters and her had left the room to put on robes, Faridah didn't think twice about her parents bringing up the anam cara. She assumed they'd tell him about the spirit and then declare that the spirit was to leave Killian be from that point forward.

"What did..." Faridah cleared her throat and began again. "What did they say to you?"

"They asked me if I was willing to change and marry you."

Faridah's hands stilled. Her cheeks felt like they were on fire and she felt at any moment she was going to be sick. Human relationships normally didn't work at a pace like mermaids. Mermaids believed in fate fiercely.

"I am so sorry, Killian," Faridah sighed. "I can take you back to the surface and explain to my parents–"

"I'd like to hear your thoughts," Killian said, turning to face her. Faridah barely heard his words because of how loud her heart was pounding. "Do you think I am your anam cara?"

"Honestly," Faridah took a deep breath. "It was Lola who brought it up to me. I hadn't considered the idea. I just knew I felt something towards you. Anam cara hadn't crossed my mind."

"But what are your thoughts now? Do you think I am this anam cara?"

"Yes. I tried to tell myself that you weren't. I thought of every possible excuse but in the end, yes. I believe we are anam caras," she blurted before she had the chance to chicken out. Killian sat frozen like a statue.

Internally, Faridah kicked herself for opening her mouth; however, in the end, she knew they needed to talk about it.

"How exactly do I get changed into one of you?" Killian sighed. "Doesn't seem humanly possible, but then again, I'm talking to a mermaid." Faridah frowned at his words and tone. "Sorry. I'm just a bit taken back by all this."

"I know. I'm sorry." Faridah's eyes began to fill with tears.

This was all her fault. If she had never gone to the loch that day, she never would have met Killian. He would be free to live his life without being put in such a hard predicament. She didn't want him to be forced to like her. She wanted him to like her because of who she was not who fate said she was.

"Faridah," Killian said softly and took hold of her hands. "Please, don't cry. We'll figure something out."

"This is all my fault," she sobbed. Killian pulled her onto his lap and wrapped his arms around her. She buried her face in his shirt and cried.

"Faridah, this isn't your fault. It's nobody's fault. So please don't cry. Okay?"

All she could do was nod and cry harder. Many emotions were hitting her at once. She didn't know whether she was coming or going. Since she left the pub, Faridah had looked forward to spending one-on-one time with Killian. She didn't think their alone time would be ordered by her father.

"Faridah. Sweetheart," Killian rubbed her back. "You're breaking my heart."

"I'm sorry," she sniffled. He kissed the top of her head.

"Don't apologize." He placed his finger under her chin and tilted her head back to where she was looking up at him. He smiled then kissed her softly. "We'll figure this all out. Promise."

"But if I wasn't a mermai–" Faridah's words were cut off by Killian's lips. He kissed her with the passion of the seven seas.

She wrapped her arms around his neck and pulled him closer to her. Their kiss deepened with their tongues exploring each other's mouths. Killian tasted of malt and cinnamon.

"Killian," she moaned into his mouth.

"So beautiful," Killian groaned and rubbed the small of her back. He nipped her bottom lip. A heat rose between her thighs. The need for Killian grew.

"Please." Faridah wasn't sure what she was pleading for... she just knew Killian had what she needed.

Killian's hand moved around to the front of Faridah. He moved her robe slowly up to her waist. She trembled with nerves and excitement. With his other hand, he held the back of her neck and kissed her in a way she had only dreamed of.

Faridah gasped when she felt something hard beneath her, between her and Killian. The thought of Killian being aroused and hard because of her. She squeezed her thighs together to dull the sudden wanton ache.

Killian rubbed Faridah's skin right above her knees. Wantonly, Faridah parted her legs slightly allowing him access to her. His body tensed and their kiss stopped briefly. He looked at her with questioning eyes.

"Are you–" he asked, but Faridah pressed a finger against his lips.

"Please," she whispered and kissed him. Killian didn't hesitate. Their kiss continued as though it had never stopped.

The kiss sent warmth, tingles, and emotions throughout Faridah's body. Countless moans escaped her mouth as the kiss continued and Killian's fingers danced their way up along the inside of her thighs. She felt like her entire world was spinning.

How can something feel so good?

"Killian, please," Faridah whimpered. He moved his kisses to the nape of her neck.

"What do you need from me, Faridah?" Killian asked, kissing up the side of her neck. Faridah's eyes closed and her head fell back exposing her neck to him in full

"More. Please. More," she gasped.

Killian picked her up swiftly and placed her in the center of the bed with her head resting on the pillows. Her hair fanned out across the pillows. Killian opened her robe exposing her body to him. His eyes roamed across her body and then settled on her eyes. He smiled.

"You're absolutely stunning, Faridah," he said huskily. Faridah blushed at the compliment and reached for the edge of the robe to close it around her. Killian held her hands. "Don't hide from me."

He helped her sit up and then took the robe off of her and tossed it across the room. Gently, he laid her back down onto the bed. He kissed the tip of her nose.

"I don't want to ever see you sad," he whispered, looking her in the eyes. "Never."

Faridah's heart swelled with warmth. Killian's words were like an elixir from the gods that washed away all her heartache, pain, and struggles. His words opened her heart, mind, and soul to the endless possibilities for her future.

"I want you to feel nothing but happiness and pleasure, Faridah." He kissed the tip of her nose again and smiled.

"I want the same for you," she whispered.

"You're sweet." He held her hip and stroked it with his finger. Faridah's back arched in response pressing her breasts against him. Killian's shirt brushed against her nipples causing a wave of heat and sensations throughout her body.

"Take yours clothes off," she moaned. "I want to feel your skin against mine."

It seemed like he moved at the speed of light. Faridah watched Killian pull his shirt up over the back of his head. He tossed it off to the side and looked down at Faridah.

Faridah looked Killian's chest over with wide eyes. He was the perfect build. His muscles were defined. Tattoos covered the right side of his body. Something shiny caught her eyes. She brought her eyes to the shiny objects.

Yum, she thought as she looked at his nipple piercings.

"What? Don't like them?" he asked, looking down at his piercings. Faridah brought her fingers up to his nipples.

"Do they hurt?"

Killian looked at her and shook his head.

"Not anymore. When I first got them, they did," he replied. Faridah sat up and kissed both of his nipples. Killian groaned and tightened his grip on her hip. She flicked one of his nipples with her tongue then circled it with her tongue.

"Damn, baby," he moaned as she moved to the other nipple and repeated her actions.

Faridah sucked on his nipple. The metal of the piercings clicked against her teeth. She liked the sound it made. With her tongue she flicked his nipple where his piercing was. Killian groaned and muttered something huskily under his breath.

"Does it feel good?" Faridah asked nervously.

"Mmhmm," he replied. Faridah sucked his nipple harder and nipped it slightly. "Fuck!" Killian roared and laid her flat on her back.

Nerves filled Faridah. She hadn't meant to hurt him. She had never been with a man and only knew of intimacy from the stories her sister shared with her.

"I'm sorr–" she began to apologize for hurting him, but he dipped his fingers between her thighs. He circled her clit with the tip of his finger. Faridah bucked wildly beneath him.

"Do you like when I touch you there?" he smirked. She nodded frantically. "What about when I touch you here?"

He slipped a finger inside her. Her body stretched to fit his finger. Faridah bit her lip to keep from screaming. She felt pain and pleasure mixed together. Two emotions she didn't think would ever be a heavenly combination.

"You're tight, Faridah," Killian groaned. "So tight."

"I'm sorry. Is that bad?" she asked faintly. Killian shook his head and chuckled.

"No, sweetheart. It's perfect."

Faridah felt like a youngling in the department of intimacy. She didn't want to turn Killian off by asking questions, but she lacked experience and wanted to be able to please him.

Killian lifted her legs straight up in the air and lay on the bed with his face inches from her heat. Faridah's eyes widened. She suddenly felt too exposed and embarrassed.

"Relax," Killian whispered. "I want to please you." He spread her legs and draped them over his shoulders. Faridah looked down between her legs to see Killian looking at her with a naughty smirk on his face.

"Oh. My," she breathed.

"You look delicious." His eyes were on her heat.

Faridah's sisters had never mentioned anything like this before. She was clueless to what was going to happen next but aroused at the same time. There were so many emotions that her body was feeling, and she couldn't steady herself on just one of them.

Faridah's hips bucked and her back arched when Killian's tongue swiped along her heat and up to her clit. She gripped the sheets and bit back a scream. The last thing she wanted was someone to interrupt them.

Killian kissed, sucked, and licked Faridah's heat. His finger worked its way in and out of her. She found it hard to breathe as she gasped from pleasure and need. She clung to the sheets for dear life while Killian worked her body as though it was his own.

CHAPTER TEN

Killian

The way Faridah's body was responding to Killian's tongue and finger made it hard for him to take things slowly. A primal urge rose from the deepest depths of him making him want to take her and make her his forever. He couldn't explain the feeling. He just knew that he wanted Faridah to be his and no one else's.

Killian buried his face between Faridah's thighs. When her thighs squeezed against his head, he grinned and slipped a second finger inside her. Her pussy stretched to fit his fingers.

Fuck, she's so tight, Killian groaned to himself.

"Killian!" she screamed. "I'm... I'm..." Her pussy tightened down around his finger.

"Come for me," he growled and flicked her clit with his tongue. She shattered. Her body quaked as her orgasm consumed her. Killian didn't let up on the speed of his fingers moving in and out of her. He licked, sucked, and nibbled at her clit.

"Fuck!" she roared.

"Princess," a group of men shouted outside the door. Killian heard the doorknob begin to turn. He panicked and went to sit up. Faridah's legs' tight hold around his neck kept him in place.

"Fuck off!" she screamed, making Killian laugh. "Go guard somewhere else! That's an order!"

"Yes, Your Highness," the group of men replied. Killian could hear the amusement in some of their voices. Heavy footsteps sounded and soon faded away.

"Are you sure you don't want me to stop?" Killian asked, holding back a laugh.

"No. Please. That felt..." Her legs trembled and she sucked in a sharp breath. "Amazing. That felt amazing."

"This?" He thrust his two fingers in and out of her fast. "Or this?" He sucked on her clit.

"All of it," she whimpered.

"Are you still feeling sad?" Killian chuckled.

"Yes. Definitely. Quite sad. Devastated."

"You're naughty," he grinned then sucked her clit back into his mouth. She screamed out in pleasure. Her legs released their hold on him and spread open. Killian brought his gaze up over her body to her face. She was looking down at him with lust-filled eyes.

He continued ramming his fingers in and out of her, while he sucked, licked, and taunted her clit with his mouth. She watched him intensely. With his movements and touches, her hips bucked, rolled, and tilted, grinding her clit against his mouth.

Killian's cock pressed firmly against the inside of his jeans. It ached to be freed. He wanted to remove his pants and stroke his cock, while he devoured Faridah's pussy. However, he didn't trust himself to leave it at that. He'd be greedy and bury every inch of his cock inside her.

He settled for shoving his free hand down his pants and stroking his cock the best he could given the lack of room. Faridah's sounds, movements, and taste made Killian feel like a madman. He wanted her like there was no tomorrow.

He stroked his cock harder and moaned against her clit.

"Let me please you," Faridah's soft words brought Killian to a halt. He lifted his head and looked at her. "I can do that for you."

Killian imagined Faridah's hand wrapped around his cock stroking him. He closed his eyes and moaned. He needed to not give in to temptation. He didn't need to ruin Faridah's life by a hasty decision.

"That sounds amazing," he opened his eyes. "But it will lead to more. A lot more."

"So?" Her cheeks reddened. "I don't mind."

"It's not that simple, beautiful," he smiled.

"Do you not want to take me?"

Killian frowned and slipped his fingers from her. He sat up on his knees, grabbed her hand and placed it on the front of his jeans. Her eyes widened.

"You did that to me," he grinned. "Of course, I want to have you."

"Then why don't you?" she asked softly.

"I don't want to ruin your life because of my horniness, Faridah."

"Neither of our lives will be ruined because of *our* horniness. I won't tell," she grinned vixen-like.

"When did you become so naughty?" Killian teased. Faridah squeezed his cock through his pants.

"When did you become so naughty?" she retorted, making him laugh.

"What do you want from me, Faridah?" Killian asked, leaning forward and stroking her cheek. She closed her eyes briefly then opened them. "Tell me, and I'll give it to you. I'll give you anything you ask of me."

Killian's words flowed from his mouth without thought. They were words with heavy promises, but he meant them. He'd give her the world if she asked for it.

"Be mine," she whispered, catching him off guard. He had expected her to reply with something involving sex.

"What?" he breathed.

"I want us." She gestured back and forth between them. "I don't want you to leave me again, Killian. Please."

Killian laid next to Faridah and pulled her into his arms. She nuzzled against his neck.

"Will you stay, if I ask you to?" she whispered.

"Yes," he replied quietly. It was a big commitment. He'd be walking away from everything he had ever known. He knew he was being hasty with his answer, but his heart had spoken.

Faridah sat up on her elbow and looked at him. She was smiling ear to ear.

"Really?" she asked excitedly. Killian laughed and then nodded. "Is this because of my parents? Or because of..." Her words died off.

"It's because of you, Faridah. No one else," he replied.

Not even a few hours ago, Killian had been filled with nerves at the thought of marrying Faridah and having children. Now, he laid beside her promising the world to her and he didn't waver. It's what he wanted deep down. He could only assume his nerves from earlier had been because of the topic being brought up by Faridah's parents – the king and queen.

"Are you asking me to stay?" Killian held Faridah's hand.

"Yes," she whispered. "Or I can go back with you, if you'd like."

"How would that work? You need the water from the loch to survive right?"

"Technically," she admitted. "Any water will do to keep me in human form."

"But..." Killian prompted.

"But the loch and my world's water is what will keep me healthy."

Killian frowned at the idea of Faridah being sick because she was away from the loch.

He took a deep breath and firmly said, "Then we will stay."

CHAPTER ELEVEN

Faridah

"Wonderful!" Faridah's mother, the queen, called out as Faridah's bedroom door opened.

"Mother!" Faridah shrieked. She yanked the sheets up over her causing Killian to lose his balance. He toppled over the side of the bed and onto the floor. "Killian!"

Faridah leaned over the side of the bed and looked down at him. He laid flat on his back looking up at the mural of Atlantis on the ceiling.

"Are you okay?" she asked. He simply nodded and then let out a heavy sigh. Faridah turned to the other side of the bed, where her mother stood by the door. The queen's ladies-in-waiting stood behind her along with the queen's guards. "Mother, now isn't really a good time."

"Oh, my," the queen laughed. "This is true. You could be using this time to bring life into this world."

"Mother!" Faridah screamed. The queen simply waved off Faridah's loud word.

"I will leave you two be. However, in the morning, we will discuss the wedding," her mother said firmly then turned to exit. She stopped after a few steps. "Killian?"

Killian poked his head up from the other side of the bed. His cheeks were red, and he looked mortified. Faridah's mother smiled.

"Remember what I said. If you help bring life into this world with Faridah, you will be forever in my favor," the queen smiled.

"Out! Out! Out!" Faridah threw a pillow with each word. The queen's guards moved to guard the queen, but the queen stopped them by holding up her hand.

"It's simply pillows," Faridah's mother laughed. "Besides, I would feel the same too, if my mother interrupted."

"Yes, Your Majesty," the guards replied.

"Faridah. Killian," the queen acknowledged them then took her leave. The door to Faridah's room closed leaving Faridah and Killian alone again.

Faridah grabbed a pillow that remained on her bed and screamed into it at the top of her lungs. Then she proceeded to whack it against the bed in an attempt to release all her frustrations.

"You okay?" Killian chuckled from his spot on the floor.

"No. I'm mortified," Faridah seethed.

"Yeah. That was a bit embarrassing," he admitted, and then stood up. "Thought we locked the door?"

"I did too," she sighed.

When they had come into the room, Faridah had been a ball of nerves. Perhaps she didn't lock the door like she had thought she had. The guards had already busted in once, and now her mother.

Faridah sighed heavily.

"Honestly, I don't think I did," she offered him an apologetic smile. "I was so nervous when we came to my room."

"Me too," Killian laughed and looked around the room.

"What are you looking for?"

"Your clothes." Faridah frowned at his words. "I think it's best if we save any more fun for... someplace else."

"Lock the door," she said huskily. Killian laughed and shook his head. Faridah crossed her arms and pouted. "Why not?"

"Because I have a feeling your dad will be coming through that door soon to discuss a wedding."

• • • •

Killian had been right. Less than five minutes after Faridah dressed, her father knocked on the door. He requested Killian's presence. Reluctantly, Killian followed the king leaving Faridah to sulk in her room.

"A bunch of bullsh–"

"Faridah Addair!" Her mother scolded from the open doorway. Faridah stood up and bowed her head slightly.

"Mother," Faridah whispered. She looked up to see her mother smiling.

"Come, daughter," her mother held out her hand for Faridah to take hold. "We're going to the Chamber of Gaoil to pray."

"Has something bad happened?" Faridah panicked.

"No. We are to announce your betrothed to the ancestors and ask for them to watch over you two as you enter marriage."

Faridah's stomach knotted as she digested her mother's words. So many emotions were rocketing through Faridah. Nerves. Excitement. Fear. Everything felt surreal. And everything seemed to be happening way too fast.

Faridah realized that her emotions regarding being with Killian for eternity were a rollercoaster. She wanted to be with him for the rest of her life, but she worried they were rushing things. On the other hand, she couldn't wait to spend the rest of her days with him because he was her anam caras.

"It is normal to be worried, Faridah," the queen said, taking Faridah's hand. "I was nervous about marrying your father."

"You were?" Faridah asked, looking at her mother. Her mother nodded then smiled.

"Of course. He was the Prince of the Seven Seas. I was nothing more than a mermaid. I held no title," her mother continued. "When your father and I crossed paths, I knew he was the one."

"But you were both of the same kind," Faridah sighed. "What if Killian regrets changing to our kind?" The question slipped past Faridah's lips without hesitation. The thought hadn't been a forethought, but it was deep in her heart. Her and Killian were from two worlds. By marrying her, Killian was walking away from the world he knew.

"He can still go to land, Faridah," her mother squeezed Faridah's hand gently.

"Really!" Faridah smiled. The queen nodded.

"Of course. Becoming one of us just means he'd be able to live here in the kingdom without us having to use magic to remove the water so he can breathe," her mother teased. "Him being here in human form, makes the rest of us like a goldfish out of its bowl."

"Mother," Faridah giggled. "We can breathe air. So how is that a good comparison?"

"I suppose it's not," the queen smiled. "However, casting spells is something I'm not comfortable having done in the kingdom."

"I understand, mother. I don't want our people to be hindered because of my relationship and the kingdom needs to be shielded in air."

"I knew you'd understand," the queen led Faridah out of the room. "Killian is a wise and kind man. I know he will understand too."

"Yes," Faridah smiled. "I know you're right."

CHAPTER TWELVE

Killian

Faridah's father – the king – had explained the traditions, expectations, and responsibilities of marrying into royalty. Her father also explained how an enchantress would cast a spell on Killian changing him from a human to one of their own. Killian had so many questions he had wanted to ask the king; however, Killian didn't have the courage to ask any of them.

Now, it was the following morning. Killian stood in the entrance way to the Colosseum of Gaoil. It was where the whole kingdom was waiting to witness the marriage of their beloved princess and the human.

"Nothing to fear," Faridah's father chuckled walking up behind Killian. Killian startled, turned on his heels to face the king, and lowered his head.

"Your Majesty," Killian stammered. The king pat Killian on the back.

"Relax or you'll keel over. Then Faridah and the queen will think I killed you," the king said. Killian smiled and he felt the tension in his body lessen. "That's more like it."

"Sorry, Your Majesty," Killian sighed then ran his hands through his hair. The king waved off Killian's words and looked through the window into the Colosseum.

"Quite the turnout," Faridah's father seemed pleased by what he saw.

"Your Majesty," a woman's voice whispered. Killian looked around the king to see a woman of light blue skin and vibrant red hair. She wore a black and gold robe.

"Ah, Empress Anneliese," the king smiled. The woman returned a smile and then looked at Killian.

"Killian, I've heard so much about you," Empress Anneliese whispered.

"Your Majesty," Killian bowed. He wasn't sure what he was supposed to call an empress. He could only hope he assumed right by calling her the title of Your Majesty.

"Empress Anneliese is the enchantress who will cast the spell on you," Faridah's father announced.

An empress and an enchantress? Is she a mermaid too? Killian wondered.

"No," Empress Anneliese laughed. "I am not a mermaid. I am Empress of a vampire kingdom."

"Vampires!" Killian's words were far from manly. Unless a deep shriek was considered manly. The empress and king shared a look and laughed.

"There is much to our mystical realms that you do not know of. Princess Faridah has lots to teach you," the empress smiled.

"I see this," Killian whispered.

Digesting the fact mermaids existed had taken Killian a while to fully accept. Now, he was being told of enchantresses and vampires.

"You're a vampire?" Killian asked without thought. The king groaned, but the empress smiled and shook her head." Sorry," Killian groaned at his rudeness.

"It's okay. My husband is a vampire emperor. I am an enchantress," the woman opened her mouth and pointed at her *normal-sized* teeth. When she closed her mouth, she smirked. "See, no fangs."

"Yes. I see," Killian smiled. "I apologize for my rudeness, Your Majesties."

"Nerves get the best of all of us, Killian," the empress walked past Killian and the king. She placed her hand on the window.

"Do you see anything that may stop this wedding?" the king asked, stepping up beside her and looking around the Colosseum.

"A challenger has arrived," she whispered, but her voice sounded unusual.

"Tiernan," the king growled. The empress nodded and lowered her hand. "Does he not know his place?"

"When has a man ever used common sense over love," the empress laughed. The king chuckled and looked over his shoulder at Killian.

"Do you wish to accept his challenge, or do you prefer we do it the easy way and I send him on his way since you are Faridah's anam cara?" the king asked.

"I've never been one to back down from a challenge, Your Majesty," Killian said, standing tall. The king and empress looked at each other and grinned. Killian had a feeling he was biting off more than he could chew, but he'd be damned if he was going to let another man take Faridah away from him.

"Since Tiernan has challenged Killian, on his wedding day. I think it is only fair that Killian be allowed to choose the type of fight," Empress Anneliese smiled.

"I agree," the king nodded and turned to Killian. "Pick your poison, Killian."

"Poison?" The color in Killian's face drained. He felt like he was going to be sick. The sudden mention of poisoning had his nerves flared once again.

"Perhaps, you can cast a spell to sedate this poor boy," the king complained.

"I supposed I could do that as a wedding present from our kingdom to yours," the empress giggled.

"Poison?" Killian repeated.

"The king is simply asking how do you want to fight? On land? In water? With arrows? With fists?" The empress' words made Killian relax and he grinned from ear to ear.

"I challenge him to an old-school fight. No weapons. Just our muscles and strength."

• • • •

Killian stood in the middle of the colosseum. The crowd had just been silenced by the king, who went and took his seat in the front row. Nerves rose in Killian. He was a professional fighter, but in this fight, he had so much more to prove and the crowd was more than just people who managed to score tickets. No. This fight was his big chance to prove himself to Faridah's parents, her kind, and to Faridah herself.

"I am glad you have accepted my challenge, human," Tiernan smirked from where he stood a few feet across from Killian. Tiernan wore no shirt displaying his muscular body and pants that would make *MC Hammer* proud.

Killian rolled his eyes.

"It was nice of you to challenge me on my wedding day," Killian rolled his eyes. "And, here I thought you might have manners."

"I'd challenge anyone for Faridah."

"Don't you already have like ten wives?" Killian remembered Faridah mentioning Tiernan and his harem of wives. It had been one of the many reasons why she hadn't married Tiernan.

"What's one more to warm my bed?" Tiernan whispered quietly to Killian.

All Killian saw at that moment was red. He launched at Tiernan and put the man in a chokehold. The crowd was on its feet. At first, the crowd was shocked, but soon they were cheering for the two contenders. One of whom was currently fighting tooth and nail to get out of Killian's hold.

"Faridah deserves more," Killian growled as he leaned back and allowed his body to drop to the ground. His arms still remained locked in position around Tiernan's neck.

"I assume he said something?" the king said, walking up to the two men.

"He thinks Faridah is nothing more than a body to warm his bed," Killian snarled between clenched teeth.

"Killian, he is turning blue," the king pointed at Tiernan's face. Killian brought his attention to Tiernan's face. The king was right. Killian had deprived Tiernan of much of his oxygen. "Release him."

Killian released his hold on Tiernan and kicked the man off him. He jumped to his feet and pointed down at Tiernan, who was now on his hands and knees gasping for air.

"Faridah will *NEVER* be yours. Ever. Next time, I will not go easy on you so mind your tongue," Killian's words spat out of his mouth like venom.

CHAPTER THIRTEEN

Faridah

Faridah's hair was nearly done when one of the guards came to the chamber to notify the queen of the chaos unfolding in the middle of the colosseum. The queen had cursed in their native tongue before heading out to deal with Tiernan. Faridah had been ordered to stay in the chamber to finish getting her hair done; however, nothing in the seven seas was going to stop her from dealing with Tiernan. He was trying to ruin her most precious day... her wedding day.

The ladies in waiting had frantically ran after Faridah as she made her way out into the colosseum. The crowd had just acknowledged the queen and taken their seat. When they saw Faridah, they stood again to acknowledge their princess. Faridah was fuming but took the time to greet those who had come to celebrate her special day.

Once she was done, she made her way over to her parents, Killian, and Tiernan. Tiernan was down on both of his knees. His hands rested on his lap and his head was lowered. Her mother was cursing him out while keeping a composed, elegant smile on her face for those spectators in the seats.

Faridah didn't want proprieties and elegancy. Tiernan had crossed a line.

"You're lucky Killian didn't kill you, Tiernan," my father smirked. Faridah looked at Killian, who was glaring down at Tiernan.

"Tiernan," Faridah whispered. Tiernan raised his head, looked at Faridah, and smiled.

Smack!

Faridah slapped him as hard as she could across the face. The colosseum fell to silence.

"How dare you try to ruin my wedding day!" she seethed. Tiernan held his face where Faridah had slapped him. "I order that you go home to your wives and never show your face to me again!"

"Faridah," Tiernan gasped. "You don't mean that."

"The hell if I don't," she growled. "I don't want to see your face ever again. Not even in the afterlife so piss off." Faridah's chest rose and lowered rapidly with each fast, heavy breath she took. Her fists were clenched at her side. She wanted to punch the arrogant jerk in the face, but she had already slapped him in front of nearly the entire kingdom.

"You heard my daughter. Piss off," the king chuckled. Tiernan looked like he wanted to say something. His eyes were locked on Faridah.

"Tiernan," the queen said smoothly. Tiernan looked at the queen. "Killian is Faridah's aman cara. You know this. The entire kingdom knows this, and yet you chose to challenge Killian on their wedding day."

"I just—"

"Shut it," the queen ordered. "Over the years, we had considered you as a husband for Faridah; however, you chose to bed nearly all the women in the kingdom and marry half of them. And, today, of all days you decide to show your as—" The queen took a deep breath. "Leave now before I smack you myself."

The smile on the queen's face never broke. Those watching would assume that the queen was speaking elegantly and saying kind words to Tiernan. Faridah admired her mother's ability to keep her temper at bay.

"Yes, Your Majesty," Tiernan replied. He stood up, and bowed his head to Faridah's parents, then Faridah before turning and walking away. Faridah wondered if Tiernan would actually stay away, but a gut feeling told her that wasn't the last she'd be seeing of him.

"You look beautiful," Killian whispered. Faridah startled. She hadn't noticed him walking up to her side.

"Thank you," she blushed. He took her hand and kissed the top of it.

"You look just as beautiful as your mother did on our wedding day," her father smiled.

"Thank you, father," Faridah smiled up at her father.

"I do believe there is a wedding to attend," Faridah's mother said sweetly as though nothing had ever happened.

"Shall I do the honors first," a woman asked. Faridah recognized the woman's voice. It was Empress Anneliese, the enchantress. Faridah turned to see the woman standing a few feet away. The woman was even more beautiful than the last time Faridah had seen her. "Hello, Your Highness."

"Hello, Your Majesty," Faridah lowered her head slightly and smiled. "I am honored for you being able to attend."

"I wouldn't miss it for the world," the empress smiled and walked over to Faridah and Killian. Faridah's father took hold of Killian's hand and Faridah's hand. He smiled at them.

"I am glad for this day," he nodded at his own words. "It is a special day when I am able to marry my daughter off to her aman cara."

Faridah felt herself getting emotional. A day she had dreamed of was finally here. To make it more special, it was Killian she was marrying. Never in a thousand years did she think she'd find her happily ever after with the boy who couldn't swim.

"Killian, are you ready to begin your new life?" Faridah's mother asked Killian. Faridah and her father looked at him.

"Yes," he said firmly.

"Good," she smiled. "Let the ceremony begin!" She shouted.

The colosseum filled with cheering and lively music began to play indicating the start of a royal wedding. Faridah's sisters walked over to her with smiles on their faces. Seeing them happy for her made the event that much more special.

"This is quite a turnout," a man said. Faridah and Killian turned to look at the man. It was Killian's cousin, George. He was wearing a tuxedo and had his hair slicked back.

"George?" Killian asked in shock.

"You didn't think I'd miss this special day, did ya, lake dreamer?" George smiled.

Killian and Faridah looked at the king, who smiled.

"I believe it is a tradition for human grooms to have a best man," the king informed the two.

"But what about the secret of your kind?" Killian whispered.

"Don't worry about that. The queen was very persuasive about me not telling a soul," George said, turning to smile at Faridah's mother.

"How did you find him?" Faridah asked. She was still confused about how George was standing in the middle of the colosseum when neither she nor Killian brought him.

"I actually found your robed fella. When Killian hadn't been seen for a while, I panicked and went looking. I was brought to the king and queen."

"And you weren't killed?" Killian asked wide-eyed.

"Obviously not, you dobber!" George shook his head. "That spirit fella is actually quite nice." Killian looked between Faridah, the king, and the queen.

"We will discuss that another time. Right now, there are more important things. Am I right?" Faridah's mother asked Killian. Killian looked at Faridah and smiled.

"Absolutely."

* * * *

The ceremony lasted for quite some time because it needed to be said in English and in Faridah's native tongue. The entire time her hand trembled beneath Killian and her father's hands. She took slow breaths in fear of passing out. She couldn't believe she was getting married. The more and more she thought about it, the more anxious she felt.

"You may kiss your bride," her father said. His voice boomed throughout the colosseum. Faridah grimaced at the loudness, but only briefly for Killian's lips captured hers.

They kissed passionately, in front of the entire kingdom. Killian didn't seem to mind having that many eyes on them, and truthfully, neither did Faridah. She wanted the whole realm to know that she was his and he was hers.

"Get a room already, will ya," George teased. Killian broke his kiss with Faridah slowly. He leaned his forehead against hers and chuckled.

"My beautiful wife," he whispered.

"My handsome husband," Faridah replied sweetly.

"I'll love you for eternity, and will stop at nothing to give you happiness, Faridah Addair-Bridgestone."

It filled Faridah's heart with joy to know she was Killian's wife, Mrs. Bridgestone—princess of the seven seas and wife of the lake dreamer.

Killian

Six months later...

Killian swam through the halls of the castle with his guards right behind him. It had taken him several days, after Empress Anneliese had cast the spell on him, to adjust to his new abilities to breathe and talk underwater. Now, he was a natural.

"Prince Consort Killian," one of the throne room guards announced as the doors to the throne room opened. Killian swam inside and to the front where the king and queen were seated in their thrones. He bowed his head.

"Your Majesties," he said before raising his head.

"Killian," Faridah's mother smiled.

"Where is Faridah?" the king asked, looking around behind Killian.

"She's a bit..." Killian grinned and thought of his next words carefully. "She's a bit under the weather."

"Is she still mad because Her Majesty sent you the gifts?" Faridah's father chuckled. The queen rolled her eyes and then laughed.

"I told you both that if—"

"Princess Faridah and Lady Adeline," a guard announced behind Killian. Killian turned to see his Faridah swimming towards him with their newborn daughter in their arms.

"Father," Faridah bowed her head at the king. "Mother," Faridah bowed to her mother.

"Hello, daughter," the queen smiled. "Are you upset with me?"

"No," Faridah shook her head. "Why would I be? It's not like I was the one who gave birth or anything?" she sassed, making her parents surprisingly laugh.

Killian wrapped an arm around Faridah's waist. He kissed the side of her head and then the top of their daughter's head.

He still couldn't believe he was a father. It all seemed to have happened at the speed of light.

I wouldn't change it for the world, he thought as he looked into his daughter's beautiful violet-colored eyes.

She was Killian's definition of perfection. Her skin was a soft caramel; a mix between Killian and Faridah's tone. She had beautiful brown curly hair. And her tail was a variety of pinks, purples, and blues.

"Faridah, I told you on your wedding day how I would favor Killian if you and he brought life into this world," the queen smiled.

"You didn't tell me how you would forget about me," Faridah pouted. Killian chuckled and kissed Faridah's cheek.

"No one could ever forget about you, my beautiful wife," he smiled.

"Hush, you," she glared at him, but her glare soon disappeared, and she laughed. "Mother. Father. I would like a day or two with Killian. Can Adeline stay here with—"

"Yes!" the king shouted, startling Adeline, who began to cry. Faridah's father swam over to the three of them and took Adeline from Faridah's arms. "I'm so sorry, my little princess. Did Grandpa frighten you?"

The king held Adeline tenderly in his arms and then swam over to his throne and took his seat once more. He baby-talked to his granddaughter and made silly faces in an attempt to make her stop crying.

Faridah's parents never ceased to amaze Killian. Her father was a great and all-mighty ruler, yet, the man would goo-goo, ga-ga in a room full of people to make his granddaughter happy. Faridah's mother was kind; however, seeing her put Tiernan in his place on Killian and Faridah's wedding day had left a lasting impression. Killian never wanted to get on her bad side. When the queen had learned of Faridah being pregnant, the queen had kept her word and favored Killian over the other sons-in-law, since they had yet to produce children.

Killian often joked with Faridah how they would need to have another child if he ever fell on bad terms with her mother. Faridah told him he would sleep elsewhere if he didn't stop mentioning them having more children to keep the queen happy. Truthfully, Killian wanted more children with Faridah regardless of the queen's happiness. Adeline and Faridah filled Killian's heart, but he was sure he could make room for one or two more in his heart.

"He's not even listening," Faridah complained. She was looking up at Killian and frowning.

"Sorry, love," he smiled. She rolled her eyes and looked at her parents.

"Perhaps, I will go to the surface on my own. He can stay here," she announced, crossing her arms in front of her chest. Killian leaned over to her ear.

"Are you sure you want to go without me, my beautiful wife?" he whispered against her ear. He watched as her body tensed and she sucked in a sharp breath. She slowly turned and faced him.

"Do you really want to spend time with me, Killian?" she asked softly.

Killian took hold of her face with both of his hands and looked her in the eyes. He kissed her forehead and then the tip of her nose.

"Of course."

"For how long?"

"Today…" he kissed her forehead. "Tomorrow." He kissed the tip of her nose. "And all eternity."

He captured her lips with his own and kissed her with all his heart. Hoping she could feel the love he felt towards her. The love he would always have for her. And, the love he would give to her for the rest of their days.

—THE END—

Don't miss out!

Visit the website below and you can sign up to receive emails whenever S.E. Isaac publishes a new book. There's no charge and no obligation.

https://books2read.com/r/B-A-RZDH-BYTOC

BOOKS 2 READ

Connecting independent readers to independent writers.

Also by S.E. Isaac

Dark Wolves Series
Caine
The Wolfe Brothers

Naughty Fairytales
The Big Bad Wolves
Little Mermaid's Tales

Standalone
Lake Dreamer